Scaredy Squirrel never sleeps.
He'd rather stay awake than risk having
a bad dream in the middle of the night.

A few creatures Scaredy Squirrel is afraid could appear in a bad dream:

dragons

fairies

WARNING!

Scaredy Squirrel insists that everyone check under their beds before reading this book.

To Joe, who dreams about getting a little more sleep

First paperback edition 2012

Text and illustrations © 2009 Mélanie Watt

Kids Can Press acknowledges the financial support of the Government of Ontario, through the Ontario
Media Development Corporation's Ontario Book Initiative; the Ontario Arts Council; the Canada
Council for the Arts; and the Government of Canada, through the CBF, for our publishing activity.

Published in Canada by
Kids Can Press Ltd.
25 Dockside Drive
Toronto, ON M5A 0B5

Published in the U.S. by
Kids Can Press Ltd.
2250 Military Road
Tonawanda, NY 14150

www.kidscanpress.com

The artwork in this book was rendered digitally in Photoshop.
The text is set in Potato Cut.

Edited by Tara Walker
Designed by Mélanie Watt and Karen Powers

The hardcover edition of this book is smyth sewn casebound.
The paperback edition of this book is limp sewn with a drawn-on cover.
Manufactured in Tseung Kwan O, NT Hong Kong, China, in 11/2015 by Paramount Printing Co. Ltd.

CM 09 0 9 8 7 6 5 4
CM PA 12 0 9 8 7 6 5 4 3 2

LIBRARY AND ARCHIVES CANADA CATALOGUING IN PUBLICATION

Watt, Mélanie, 1975–
     Scaredy Squirrel at night / by Mélanie Watt.

ISBN 978-1-55453-288-9 (bound)   ISBN 978-1-55453-705-1 (pbk.)

I. Title.

PS8645.A88S2826 2012   jC813'.6   C2011-907935-6

Kids Can Press is a Corus™ Entertainment company

Scaredy Squirrel
at night

by Mélanie Watt

KIDS CAN PRESS

ghosts

unicorns

vampire bats

polka-dot monsters

So he's very determined to stay awake
by keeping busy all through the night.

SCAREDY'S NIGHTTIME "TO DO" LIST

1. Count stars
(should keep you occupied for a while)

2. Play cymbals
(loud, annoying noise is sure to keep you wide awake)

3. Take up scrapbooking
(keeps you well-organized and productive)

So night
after night ...

after
night ...

after
night ...

Scaredy
avoids
sleeping.

BUT ...

...and exhaustion!

That's when Scaredy Squirrel comes face-to-face with something very alarming ...

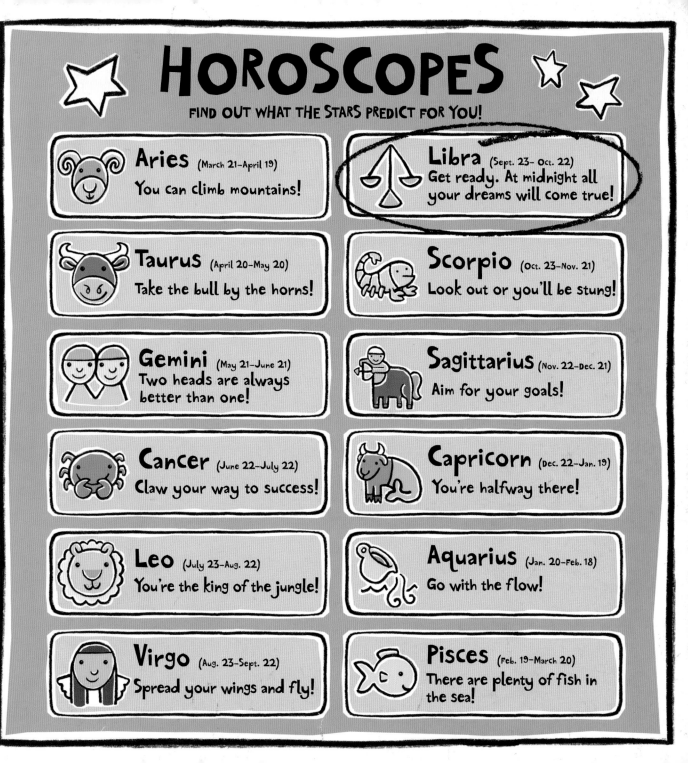

A few things
Scaredy Squirrel
needs to face his
bad dreams:

spotlight

cupcakes

banana peels

fire
extinguisher

safety cones

fan

teddy bear
(decoy)

sign

pillow and blanket

molasses

BAD DREAM ACTION PLAN

Dragons are a huge fire hazard so keep extinguisher in tree!

Not a fan of ghosts? Start the breeze and they'll be blown away!

Molasses will slow down a unicorn in a sticky situation.

Place sign upside down so bats can read it.

DO NOT DISTURB

Fairies have a sweet tooth — distract them with cupcakes!

Polka-dot monsters can't spot banana peels. Watch them slip and slide!

I am here.

Creatures think I am sleeping here.

 IMPORTANT: These creatures avoid light. Hide behind spotlight, switch it on at midnight and creatures will disappear! Remember, if all else fails, **PLAY DEAD** until sunrise.

So Scaredy Squirrel gets into position.
As he counts down to midnight, his bad
dreams seem to come true, one by one.

But when he turns on the spotlight ...

Scaredy Squirrel panics!

He steps in the molasses ...

He stumbles over a safety cone ...

8 hours later, Scaredy Squirrel finally wakes up.

... and clear thinking!

Scaredy Squirrel forgets all about his bad dreams. He realizes they were just in his imagination and nothing horrible happened in the night.

A good sleep has inspired him to get rid of a few things and replace his horoscope with something much more trustworthy ...